IMAGINE THAT

Licensed exclusively to Imagine That Publishing Ltd
Tide Mill Way, Woodbridge, Suffolk, IP12 1AP, UK
www.imaginethat.com
Copyright © 2019 Imagine That Group Ltd
All rights reserved
0 2 4 6 8 9 7 5 3 1
Manufactured in China

Retold by Georgina Wren
Illustrated by Lucy Barnard

ISBN 978-1-78958-308-3

A catalogue record for this book is available from the British Library

The Ugly Duckling

Hans Christian Andersen

Retold by Georgina Wren
Illustrated by Lucy Barnard

It was summer in the country. The wheat was golden, the trees were green and the sky was bright blue. Hidden among the reeds, a duck sat on her nest, waiting for her eggs to hatch.

At last the first egg opened and a little duckling popped out.
It was yellow, fluffy and very, very cute.

Four more eggs opened, and four more little ducklings appeared, each yellower, fluffier and cuter than the last! Finally, there was just one egg left. It was a very big egg!

After one more day, the final egg opened, and the last duckling popped out. He was grey, scruffy and much bigger than the other ducklings. 'What an enormous duckling!' said the mother duck in amazement.

The mother duck proudly took her ducklings to show the farmyard animals. But the animals were mean to the big duckling. 'He's so big and ugly!' they laughed.

Each day was the same, the last duckling was chased, teased and pushed by the other animals in the farmyard. Even the girl who fed the chickens teased him. 'You're such an ugly duckling!' she laughed.

At last the poor duckling decided to run away.

Up in the hills, the duckling met
some wild ducks on a quiet pond.
'You can stay here with us,' said the
wild ducks, 'but you are very ugly!'

Suddenly the peaceful pond was noisy with the sound of barking dogs.

The wild ducks flew off at once. The frightened duckling hid until the noise had stopped, and then ran away as fast as he could.

Just as the sun was setting, the duckling found a cottage and sneaked inside. A friendly old lady lived there with a mean cat and a bossy hen. 'If you want to stay here,' clucked the bossy hen, 'you'll need to learn to purr or lay eggs.'

'I think I should leave,' said the duckling. 'Yes, I think you probably should,' yawned the mean cat, licking his paws.

Autumn came and the leaves in the forest turned orange and gold. The duckling was sad and all alone.

One evening, he saw a flock of beautiful birds flying above the pond. 'What lovely birds!' he thought. 'I wish I could fly away with them!'

Winter arrived in the forest. The air grew colder and snow drifted down from the sky.

The poor duckling had to paddle around and around just to stop the pond from icing over completely.

One morning, the lonely duckling
felt the sun on his feathers and
heard songbirds singing in the trees.
Winter was finally over.

That day, the duckling saw three beautiful white swans on the far side of the pond. He swam over to meet them. 'I expect they'll be mean to me, just like the other animals,' he thought.

But when the swans saw the duckling, they rushed towards him, shaking their tails and honking happily.

'Don't you think I'm ugly?' asked the duckling. 'Ugly?' honked one of the swans. 'You're not ugly, you're beautiful! Look at your reflection in the water.'

And what did he see in the clear water below?

He was no longer an ugly duckling ...

... he was a beautiful swan!